# Maxine Trottier

# Rajka Kupesic

# Claire's Gift

D1311731

Scholastic Canada Ltd.

Toronto  New York  London  Auckland  Sydney
Mexico City  New Delhi  Hong Kong

*For Kelly and Kristin.*
*— M.T.*

*This book is dedicated*
*to my two wonderful sons,*
*Boris and Adrian, who are*
*my greatest sources of inspiration.*
*— R.K.*

The paintings for this book were created in oil on linen.

This book was designed in QuarkXPress, with type set in 17 point Berkeley Medium.

**Scholastic Canada Ltd.**
175 Hillmount Road, Markham, Ontario L6C 1Z7, Canada

**Scholastic Inc.**
555 Broadway, New York, NY 10012, USA

**Scholastic Australia Pty Limited**
PO Box 579, Gosford, NSW 2250, Australia

**Scholastic New Zealand Limited**
Private Bag 94407, Greenmount, Auckland, New Zealand

**Scholastic Ltd.**
Villiers House, Clarendon Avenue, Leamington Spa,
Warwickshire CV32 5PR, UK

**National Library of Canada Cataloguing in Publication Data**

Trottier, Maxine
Claire's gift

ISBN 0-439-98860-8

I. Kupesic, Rajka  II. Title.

PS8589.R685C53 2002          jC813'.54          C2001-902633-1
PZ7.T7532C1 2002

6 5 4 3 2 1          Printed in Canada          02 03 04 05

In Chéticamp the ladies hook rugs. They are beautiful things of soft wool with delicate flowers and vines twining upon them, pink and green and soft yellow as pale as winter butter. They learn the hooking when they are very small, the ladies of Chéticamp. There is a right way to hook and a wrong way, and it can take a lifetime to learn the difference. But if you do it well, then a little piece of your heart is tucked in there with the wool. That is what they say in Chéticamp.

There in Chéticamp, in a house that looked over the gulf, Tante Marie had hooked those rugs all her life. Everyone in the village called her *ma tante,* even if she was not their aunt.

"*Bonjour, ma tante!*" the children would shout as they walked by her house on their way to school, all bundled up against the cold gulf wind.

*"Bonjour, ma tante!"* the priest would call as he hurried to somewhere important, his cassock flapping around his legs.

*"Bonne nuit, ma tante,"* the young couples would whisper as they walked past her moonlit house after the dance, fiddle music still ringing in their heads.

Tante Marie lived alone in her big house; all her family had passed on or left the island. There were Christmas gifts and birthday cards from people who lived far away. When a niece or nephew had a child, Tante Marie would send over a rug and they would send back pictures. The last child had been a little girl called Claire. Her large blue eyes stared out from photographs on the mantel.

Surrounded by the pictures, Tante Marie sat alone in her parlour, and the endless hook and pull of the wool through the rugs was a soft sigh in the quiet rooms.

Then one day a letter arrived. This is what it said:

*Dear Tante Marie,*

*We have never met, but you sent me a lovely hooked rug when I married your great-nephew Paul. You sent another one when our baby Claire was born seven years ago. Well, now Paul went off to the war last year and I am all alone with Claire. I must go to work in the fish packing plant. I thought it would be nice if Claire came over to visit you for the summer. She will arrive on my cousin Jean's fish boat next week.*

*Thank you, your niece Anne*

And so Claire came to the island to spend the summer with Tante
Marie. What excitement it created! Someone would have to go to the
dock to pick her up and bring her home.

What would she look like now, this girl, the daughter of Paul who was Tante Marie's great-nephew? *Pauvre petite,* poor little thing, to have the father gone to war and the mother working in the fish packing plant. The entire village would take her in.

But Claire, the daughter of Paul, turned out to be a small silent girl with wild yellow hair who glared at everyone who came near her. Surely it was because she missed her mama, but still she might smile now and again.

*"Bienvenue, Claire,"* said Tante Marie when the child arrived, but Claire only stood in the doorway in her sweater that was a little too small and her dress that was a little too big.

The days passed slowly. Claire might wander out into the yard and watch the ocean.

*"Bonjour, ma tante! Bonjour, Claire!"* the children would shout from the gate. "Come and play!" But Claire would not.

For once in her life Tante Marie's hook lay still on the wooden table next to an unfinished rug. All she could think of was the sad little girl.

*"Bonjour, ma tante. Bonjour, Claire,"* the priest would say as Claire and Tante Marie walked down the steps of the church after mass. "And how is our girl today?" But Claire only hurried down the street, wild hair flying, back to the old house.

*"Bonsoir, ma tante. Bonsoir, Claire,"* whispered the young couples passing by after the Saturday night dance. Claire of course did not hear, for she was in her bed, having cried herself to sleep as she did every night.

Tante Marie did not know what to do. None of the nieces or nephews who had visited over the years had ever behaved in such a way. There would be a little homesickness and then it would disappear. Children loved the old house and the deep blue gulf water beyond it. They flew kites and ran in the fields and made friends with the Chéticamp children.

It was a mystery.

Finally one night, sighing and worried, Tante Marie did the only thing she could do. She picked up her rug and began to hook. The pattern of the work soothed her heart.

*With the hook catch the wool.*
*Give it just a little pull.*
*Give the wool a little tug*
*with the hook to make the rug.*

Tante Marie remembered far back when she had been a little girl herself with wild red hair. Her own Tante Émilie had taught her that rhyme the summer she set the hook in her hand.

Then Tante Marie looked up suddenly. There in the doorway stood Claire in a nightgown that was a little too worn. Tante Marie paused, the hook in her hand.

"I can tell that you are asking yourself what it is I am doing," said Tante Marie. Claire said nothing.

"Well, I am hooking a rug," said Tante Marie gently. "Would you like to see how it is done?"

Claire did not answer, but she came closer.

"It goes this way," said Tante Marie, and Claire came even closer:

*"With the hook catch the wool.*
*Give it just a little pull.*
*Give the wool a little tug*
*with the hook to make the rug."*

"May I try?" asked Claire softly. Tante Marie smiled to herself. She put the hook into Claire's hand and let her pull a few strands of wool through the squares. Claire looked up at Tante Marie and they both laughed.

"Tomorrow you will begin your own rug," said Tante Marie, "but now it is time for bed."

All that summer Claire worked on the rug. At first her work was
crooked and she had to begin again. Then, in time, the surface of the
rug smoothed out and the lines of wool were straight and even. On
rainy days they would sit in the parlour together, each of them
hooking their rugs.

When it was fine and warm they sat outside on the front porch. Everyone in Chéticamp knew about Claire's rug and wondered just what it would look like when she was finished.

Tante Marie worked quickly with her old sure hands. Claire worked very slowly so she would not make any mistakes.

"*Bonjour, Claire et ma tante,*" all the children would call as they raced by. They were sure Claire's rug would be all kites and green fields.

"*Bonjour, Claire et ma tante,*" the priest would say as he hurried by to the church. He was certain the rug would show the church itself, tall and dignified against the island sky.

"*Bonne nuit, Claire et ma tante,*" the young couples would whisper as they strolled past the house under the full moon after the dance was finished. They knew for sure that Claire's rug would have wedding rings and hearts all over it.

Then one day a letter came. This is what it said:

*Dear Tante Marie,*

*I have good news. Your great-nephew Paul will be coming home in a few weeks and I will be leaving my job at the fish plant. My cousin Jean will sail over for Claire next week. It will be good to have her home.*

*Thank you, your niece Anne*

"You will see your mama and papa again," said Tante Marie after she read the letter to Claire. "That will be a happy day for you."

"I will miss you," said Claire quietly.

"Of course you will, *ma petite,* and I will miss you also," answered Tante Marie.

The next week all of Chéticamp came to Tante Marie's fence to say farewell to Claire. With her little bag and her rug rolled under her arm she smiled and waved to everyone and said goodbye to them all. Finally Claire turned to Tante Marie.

"Now do not forget," said Tante Marie very seriously.

"I won't forget," answered Claire and she repeated:
*"With the hook catch the wool. Give it just a little pull.
Give the wool a little tug with the hook to make the rug."*

"*Parfait*," said Tante Marie. "*Bon voyage, Claire.*"

"*Au revoir, ma tante,*" answered Claire as Tante Marie
gave her a quick hug.

Tante Marie went back to her quiet life in the big house. The endless hook and pull of the wool through the rug was again a soft sigh in the quiet rooms. True, there were Christmas gifts and birthday cards from people who lived far away. But now there were letters from Claire that came every month all through the long winter.

Then one day a package arrived. In it was a letter from Claire. This is what it said:

*Dear Tante Marie,*

*Papa says you send rugs to everyone, so here is a rug for you. Mama helped me finish it. I had fun at your house last summer. May I come back again? I hope you like the rug.*

*Love, Claire*

Tante Marie opened the package. There was Claire's rug. In its centre, surrounded by twining vines and flowers, was a big white house standing against the blue of the gulf. Tante Marie could see an old woman and a small girl with wild yellow hair sitting in the sunshine on the front porch. They were both hooking rugs.

Tante Marie hung the rug in a place of honour in her parlour. All the people in Chéticamp came to see it and they all agreed that it was beautiful. Everyone knew that there was a right way to hook and a wrong way, and it might take a lifetime to learn the difference. Claire had made a good beginning. It was easy to see that a little piece of her heart was tucked in there with the wool.

That is what they said in Chéticamp and, inside her own heart, Tante Marie knew it was true.